Babies Come From God!

By Ella Sullivan

Blessed Books

Blessed Books

Faith's mommy
is going to have a baby.
Faith is going to be
a **BIG** sister.

Faith has a **BIG** question.

"Where do babies come from?"

That is a **BIG** question!
Faith's mommy thinks about
how to answer it.

She decides to tell Faith the <u>truth</u>.

"Babies come from GOD!"

Faith thinks she understands.

"Do babies come from GOD'S love?"

Faith does understand.
Her mommy is proud of her.

Mommy tells Faith how babies
come from GOD'S love.

"Yes Faith, GOD made us
male and female so that we
could fall in love and get married.

When a man and a woman
like each other they start to
spend lots of time together
to see if they are called
by GOD towards marriage."

Mommy explains to Faith how
a married man and woman
make a baby.

"After a man and a woman
are married they try
to grow their new family
with a baby.

GOD made men and women
to fit together
in a loving embrace
that creates
the miracle of new life!"

Faith has more **BIG** questions.

"But how does that work?
Can men have babies too?
Does the baby fall from the sky?"

Mommy tells Faith the <u>truth</u>.

"Babies do not fall from the sky, they grow in their mother's <u>uterus</u>.

Only women can have babies because men do not have a uterus!"

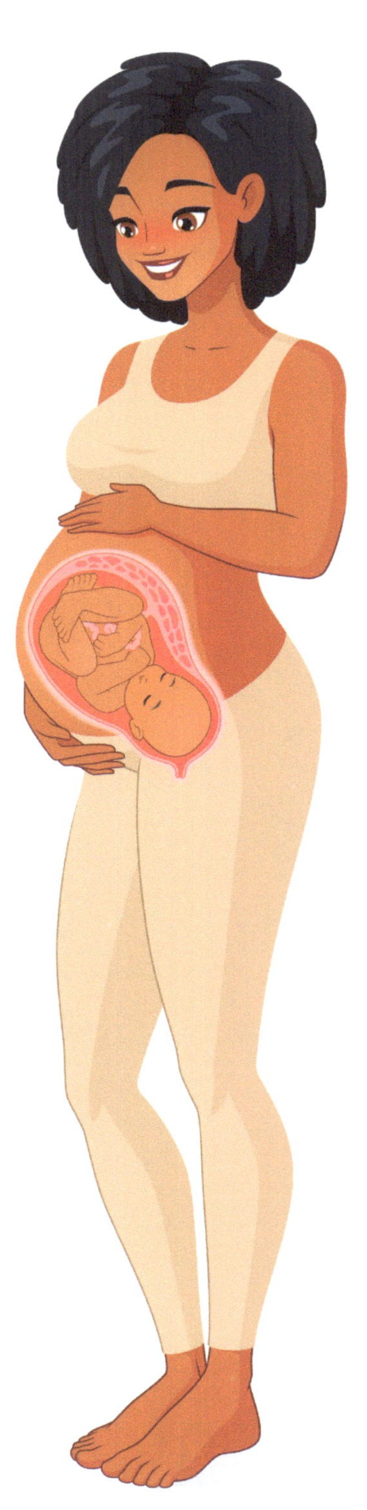

Mommy explains further.

"During the loving marital embrace,
a part of the man
and a part of the woman
join together.
At that moment
a blessed new life is formed."

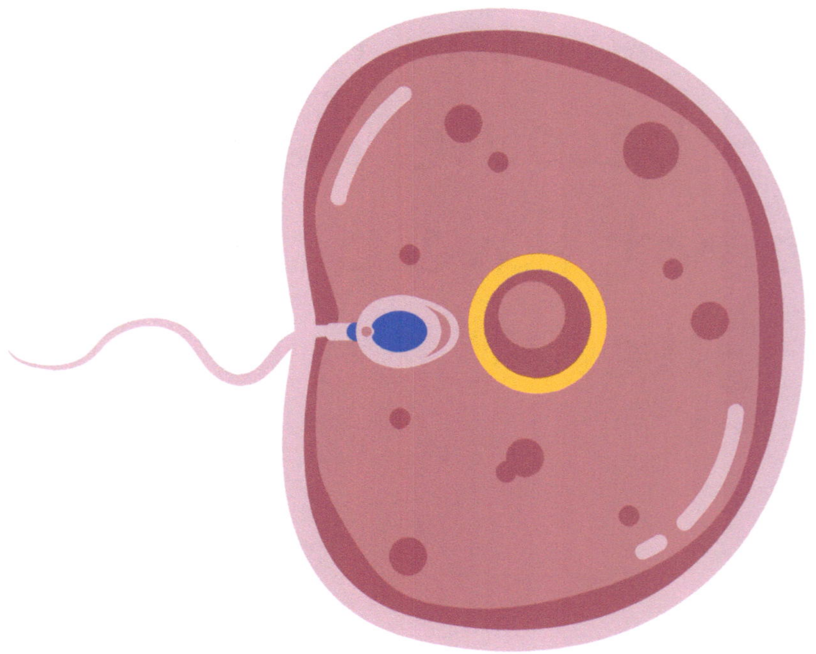

That moment is called <u>conception</u>.

The part from the man is called <u>sperm</u> and it has all the information inside it to make the new baby resemble their father.

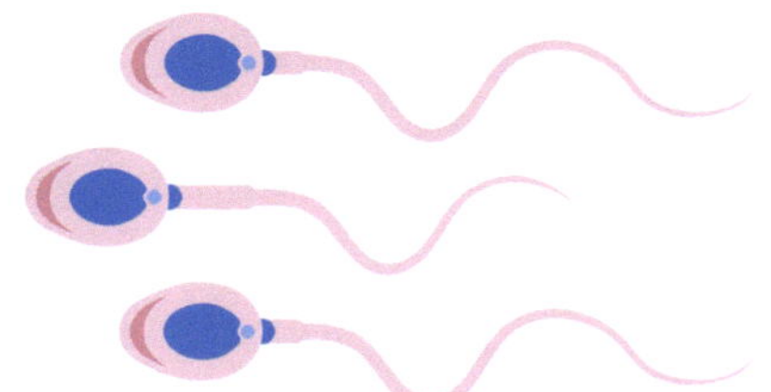

The part from the woman is called the <u>ovum</u> and it has all the information inside it to make the new baby resemble their mother.

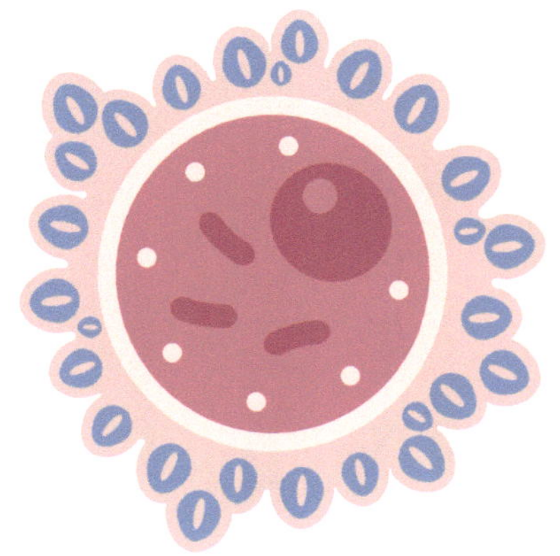

The <u>uterus</u> is the perfect first home for a baby.

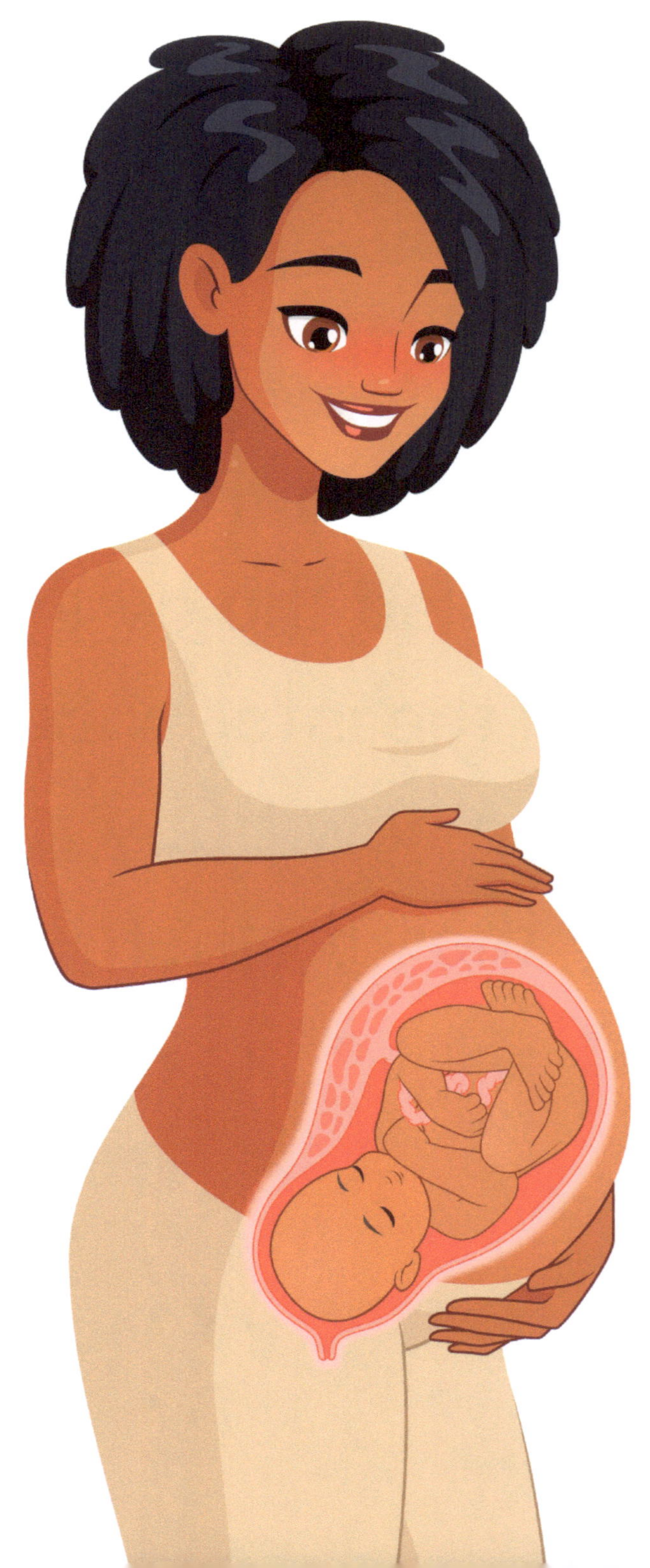

The <u>uterus</u> is warm and safe.
It meets all of the
new baby's needs.

For 9 months, the new baby
GROWS and **GROWS**
until it is ready to be born!

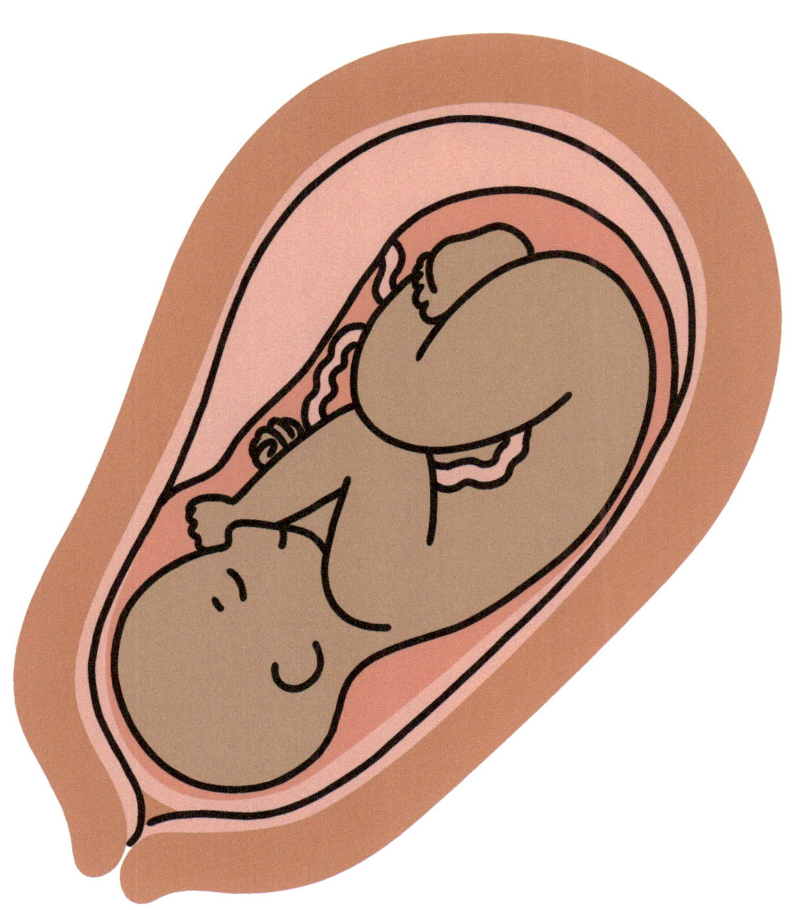

Now Faith knows
where babies come from.

"Wow! Babies really are a miracle
that come from GOD'S love.

The mommy and daddy
must feel so blessed."

Mommy tells Faith she is right.

"Yes Faith, they do feel blessed. That is how daddy and I felt when GOD gave us you."

Faith feels blessed too!
GOD has given her a loving family.
The new baby growing safely
in their mother's <u>uterus</u>
will add to that love!

Babies are a sign of **GOD'S** love!

Faith has a new question.
"Will the new baby be
a boy or a girl?"

Maybe the baby will be a **girl**
who loves to dance,
just like Faith
and her mommy.

Or, maybe
the baby will be a **boy**
who loves to play basketball,
just like Faith's daddy.

Faith's mommy tells her that she doesn't know if the new baby will be a **boy** or a **girl** yet.

Her daddy and mommy want to wait for the baby to be born to find out.

Faith's parents want it to be a
SURPRISE!

If the baby is a **girl**,
they will be thankful.

If the baby is a **boy**,
they will be thankful.

Because all babies are
gifts from **GOD**.

When the new baby is born,
the <u>doctor</u>
looks at it and announces:

"Congratulations!
you have a healthy
baby boy!"

After 9 months,
Faith meets her new
baby brother.

His name is Jonah.
That is a Bible name.
It means 'Truthful'.

Jonah is a **BOY!**
He is a gift from **GOD**.

Faith loves Jonah.
One day, mommy
will tell him that
babies come from

GOD!

Glossary

Conception 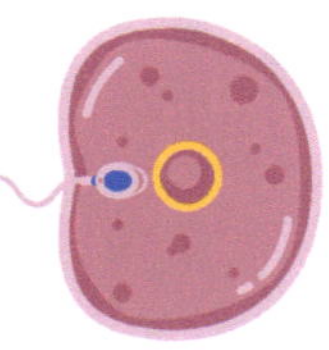

The moment when the sperm from the father and ovum from the mother join to create a new life.

Sperm 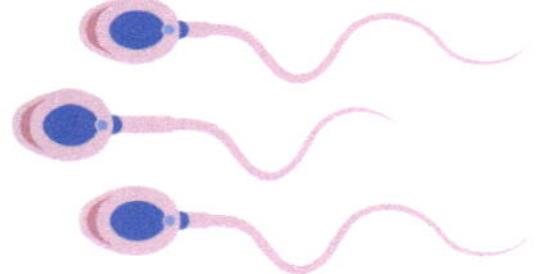

The human male's cell, which when joined with an ovum, forms a new person.

Ovum 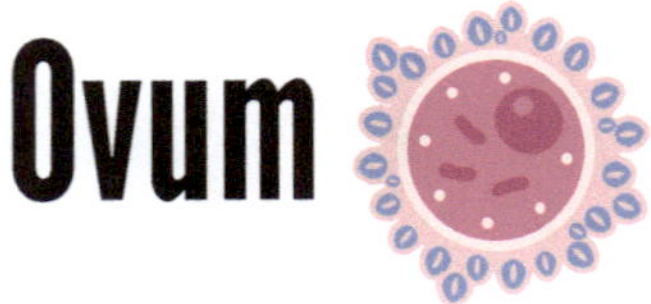

The human female's cell, which when joined with a sperm, forms a new person.

Boy

A young human male.

Girl

A young human female.

Mother

A female parent.

Father

A male parent.

Uterus 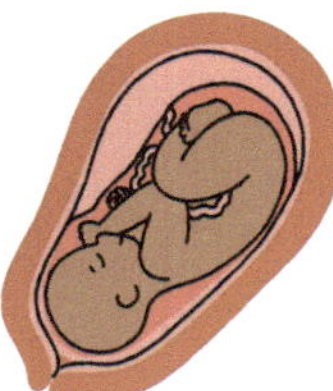

The baby's first home where it grows. It is a hollow, pear-shaped organ inside an adult female's body.